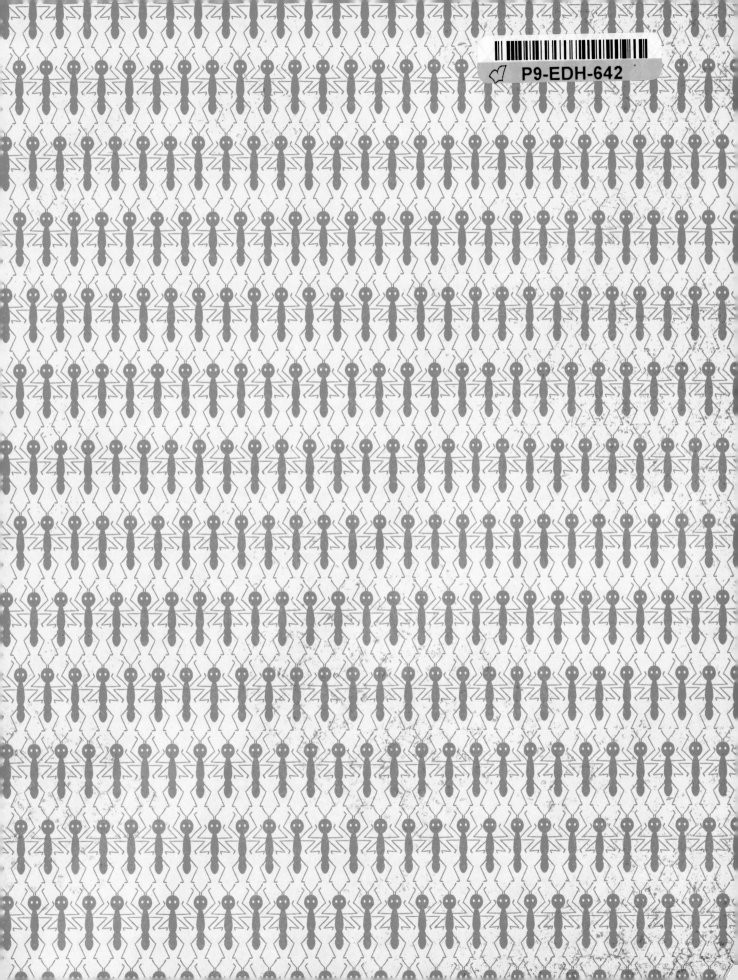

CUENTO
DE LUZ

For June Magro,
because in the smallest things are the greatest stories.

- Baltasar Magro -

This book is printed on **Stone Paper** with silver **Cradle to Cradle™** certification. Cradle to Cradle™ is one of the most demanding ecological certification systems, awarded to products that have been conceived and designed in an ecologically intelligent way.

Cradle to Cradle™ recognizes that environmentally safe materials are used in the manufacturing of Stone Paper which have been designed for re-use after recycling. The use of less energy in a more efficient way, together with the fact that no water, trees nor bleach are required, were decisive factors in awarding this valuable certification.

The Ants' Secret
Text © 2019 Baltasar Magro
Illustrations © 2019 Dani Padrón
This edition © 2019 Cuento de Luz SL
Calle Claveles, 10 | Urb. Monteclaro | Pozuelo de Alarcón | 28223 | Madrid | Spain
www.cuentodeluz.com
Title in Spanish: *El secreto de las hormigas*
English translation by Jon Brokenbrow
First printing
Printed in PRC by Shanghai Chenxi Printing Co., Ltd. March 2019, print number 1673-2
ISBN: 978-84-16733-48-4